W9-CMI-818

NIAGARA FALLS PUBLIC LIBRARY

Fall

A Level Two Reader

By Cynthia Klingel and Robert B. Noyed

The Child's World®

2

Fall is here! Fall is a season. Another name for this season is autumn. Fall comes after summer and before winter.

The sun sets earlier in the day. The air is warm during the day and cool at night.

The leaves on many trees change color. The leaves turn red, orange, and yellow. Soon the leaves will fall from the trees.

Most plants stop growing in the fall. The vegetables in the garden are ready to pick. The pumpkins have grown large and are bright orange.

Apples are also ready in the fall. It is fun to pick apples in the orchard.

Fall is always a busy time for many animals. They are getting ready for winter. Squirrels gather food to save for the winter.

There are many birds in the sky. They are flying south for the winter.

Farmers planted seeds in the spring. Now their crops are ready to harvest.

Leaves cover the ground. Some people rake the leaves into piles. Children love to jump in the leaves.

Summer is gone. Fall is here.

Soon it will be winter.

Index

To Find Out More

Books

Fowler, Allan. *How Do You Know It's Fall?* Chicago: Children's Press, 1992.

Hirschi, Ron, and Thomas D. Mangelsen (photographer). *Fall.* New York: Cobblehill Books, 1991.

Schweninger, Ann. *Autumn Days.* New York: Viking, 1991.

Web Sites

Why Leaves Change Color
http://www.esf.edu/pubprog/brochure/leaves/leaves.htm
An explanation of what happens to trees during autumn.

Note to Parents and Educators

Welcome to The Wonders of Reading™! These books provide text at three different levels for beginning readers to practice and strengthen their reading skills. Additionally, the use of nonfiction text provides readers the valuable opportunity to *read to learn*, not just to learn to read.

These leveled readers allow children to choose books at their level of reading confidence and performance. Level One books offer beginning readers simple language, word choice, and sentence structure as well as a word list. Level Two books feature slightly more difficult vocabulary, longer sentences, and longer total text. In the back of each Level Two book are an index and a list of books and Web sites for finding out more information. Level Three books continue to extend word choice and length of text. In the back of each Level Three book are a glossary, an index, and a list of books and Web sites for further research.

State and national standards in reading and language arts emphasize using nonfiction at all levels of reading development. The Wonders of Reading™ fill the historical void in nonfiction material for the primary grade readers with the additional benefit of a leveled text.

About the Authors

Cindy Klingel has worked as a high school English teacher and an elementary teacher. She is currently the curriculum director for a Minnesota school district. Writing children's books is another way for her to continue her passion for sharing the written word with children. Cindy Klingel is a frequent visitor to the children's section of bookstores and enjoys spending time with her many friends, family, and two daughters.

Bob Noyed started his career as a newspaper reporter. Since then, he has worked in communications and public relations for more than fourteen years for a Minnesota school district. He enjoys writing books for children and finds that it brings a different feeling of challenge and accomplishment from other writing projects. He is an avid reader who also enjoys music, theater, traveling, and spending time with his wife, son, and daughter.

Published by The Child's World®, Inc.
PO Box 326
Chanhassen, MN 55317-0326
800-599-READ
www.childsworld.com

Photo Credits
© 1995 Adam Jones/Dembinsky Photo Assoc. Inc.: 6
© Art Gurmankin/Unicorn Stock Photos: cover
© C.W. Beidel, M.D./Photri, Inc.: 2
© Dale Durfee/Tony Stone Images: 21
© 1996 Dan Dempster/Dembinsky Photo Assoc. Inc.: 18
© 1996 Darrell Gulin/Dembinsky Photo Assoc. Inc.: 17
© D. Young-Wolff/PhotoEdit: 10
© Jim Stamates/Tony Stone Images: 14
© Laurie Campbell/Tony Stone Images: 13
© Peter Correz/Tony Stone Images: 5
© 1999 Stan Osolinski/Dembinsky Photo Assoc. Inc.: 9

Project Coordination: Editorial Directions, Inc.
Photo Research: Alice K. Flanagan

Copyright © 2001 by The Child's World®, Inc.
All rights reserved. No part of this book may be
reproduced or utilized in any form or by any means
without written permission from the publisher.
Printed in the United States of America.

Library of Congress Cataloging-in-Publication Data
Klingel, Cynthia Fitterer.
Fall / by Cynthia Klingel and Robert B. Noyed.
p. cm. — (Wonder books)
Includes index.
Summary: Simple text describes the season of autumn, the changes the Earth
goes through, and the effects that can be seen on plants, animals, and people.
ISBN 1-56766-811-9 (lib. reinforced)
1. Autumn—Juvenile literature.   [1. Autumn.]
I. Noyed, Robert B.   II. Title.   III. Wonder books (Chanhassen, Minn.)

QB637.7 .K55   2000
508.2—dc21   99-057451

24

NIAGARA FALLS PUBLIC LIBRARY

OCT 2 0 2001

J 508.2 Kli

Fall.
Klingel, C.

PRICE: $20.13 (ONF/jn/v)